To Mary Beth and Liam,

and the mess that living makes

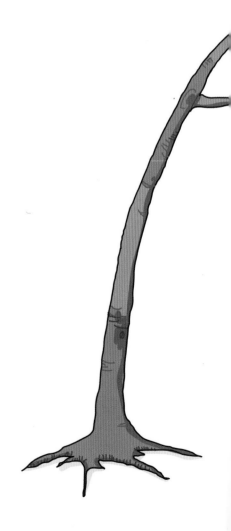

dirtball pete

eileen brennan

Random House 🏠 New York

dirtball Pete looked like something the cat dragged in.

It was a fact.

His mom said so, and his aunt Marion agreed.

Dirtball Pete also stunk to high heaven. This was another fact.

His sister, Amanda, said so, and her friend Janine totally agreed.

On any other day, this might be okay. In fact, it might be quite normal. But it wasn't just any other day.

It was THE FIFTY STATES AND WHY THEY'RE GREAT! day at school, and Dirtball Pete had a speech to recite.

Dirtball Pete's mother had a lot of reasons to worry about
this, but she also had a plan.

The girls giggled on the sofa as Dirtball Pete was marched past,
and they smirked on the stairs listening to the hot water run, and they
ha-ha'ed in the hallway as his mother's voice echoed off the tiled walls
of the bathroom–

"Now listen here, young man. Today is a very special day. Once I find you under all this dirt, I'm going to scrub you clean, and you're going to *stay* clean until the final curtain. I'm going to leave that auditorium proud of you. Do you understand?"

Dirtball Pete uttered a soap-bubbly "YES." His mother said no more and began whistling a little song to the rhythm she made with the scrub brush.

Dirtball Pete looked like a million bucks. This was a fact, and quite a surprising fact at that. His mother and Aunt Marion and Amanda and Janine all agreed.

Even his dog, Jack, was impressed.

But strangely, the closer they got to Dirtball Pete,
the more suspicious they grew.

He *looked* squeaky clean, yes, but *what* was that smell?!

"Oh, no!" his mother said. "Pet ferrets must stay home!"
So Dirtball Pete hugged Eggroll good-bye . . . for now.

Then his mother helped him into his costume.

"Dirtball Pete," his mother said, "you are the handsomest Pennsylvania ever!"

And though no one had ever really seen one before, they all knew it was true.

Jack loved his buddy Dirtball Pete. But somehow, every time
he tried to show him that,
something

bro ke.

So when Jack came running out to the car to say good-bye, Dirtball Pete's mother and Aunt Marion acted fast. They grabbed Dirtball Pete quicker than you can say "muddy dog paws" and slid him into the back of the station wagon.

And with a stomp on the gas pedal, they were off to the school recital.

For THE FIFTY STATES AND WHY THEY'RE GREAT! day, each child had prepared a little speech with facts about a different state.

As they drove to school, Dirtball Pete stared at the ceiling of the station wagon and quietly rehearsed his speech over and over again. His leaf collection made quite a comfy pillow.

With one final tidying, then a big kiss, then a quick swipe of a tissue to remove the kiss, then one last smoothing of his hair, Dirtball Pete's mother left him at the flagpole with his classmates and his teacher.

All his friends were there in state-shaped costumes, too. Yes indeed, this was not just any other day.

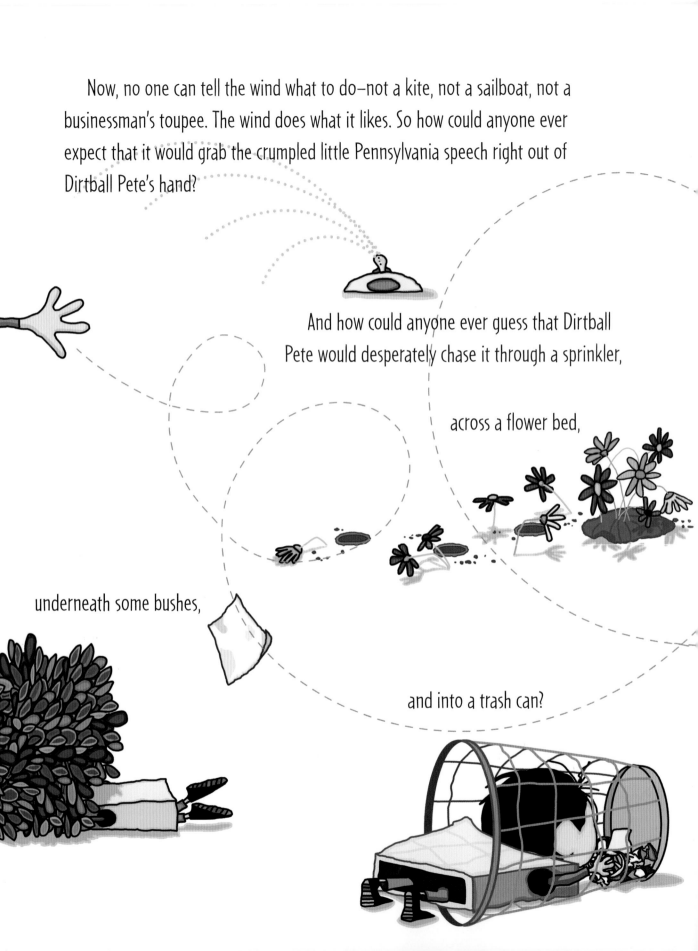

Now, no one can tell the wind what to do—not a kite, not a sailboat, not a businessman's toupee. The wind does what it likes. So how could anyone ever expect that it would grab the crumpled little Pennsylvania speech right out of Dirtball Pete's hand?

And how could anyone ever guess that Dirtball Pete would desperately chase it through a sprinkler,

across a flower bed,

underneath some bushes,

and into a trash can?

And who could ever imagine that by the time he caught it—after all that cleaning and scrubbing—Dirtball Pete would look just like . . . Dirtball Pete?!

Not Dirtball Pete, that's for sure.
In fact, he didn't even notice.

Dirtball Pete happily joined his friends, all lined up and ready to go onstage.

And just in time. The line was starting to move.

But when Dirtball Pete took his place onstage, all soggy
and damaged and stained, a round of gasps and murmurs went
through the audience.

Dirtball Pete looked like a scraggly weed in a vase of flowers.
It was a fact. His mother sighed as the whispering audience agreed.
She had wanted the world to see what a special and beautiful boy
he was underneath all that dirt.

The recital began. It started with A for Alabama, and then Alaska, and so on. State by state, one by one, each small head peered from a crisp cardboard costume, whispering facts about Kansas or Kentucky, mumbling details about Oklahoma or Oregon.

"Awww!" went the audience after each speech . . . even though most of the parents couldn't hear what their child had said.

CLOP

SQUISH!

CLOP

SQUISH!

Then it was Dirtball Pete's turn.

He took center stage, smiling into the silence.

"I am PENNSYLVANIA!" he boomed. "I was the home of the Lenape and Shawnee Indians!" he declared. "I became a state in 1787!" He stood tall.

"And my capital is Harrisburg!"

These were all facts, and Dirtball Pete said them with the loudest and clearest voice of all.

The silence in the audience turned to *hmmm*s, then to smiles, then to applause.

Dirtball Pete's mom was so proud. She thought he had delivered his lines beautifully. She said so, and Aunt Marion and Amanda and Janine and everyone in the audience agreed. They *did* see and hear and realize that underneath all that dirt, there was a very special boy.

And *that* was a fact.

a frederator
mixed media group
company

www.boldermedia.com

Visit us on the Web! www.randomhouse.com/kids

Educators and librarians, for a variety of teaching tools, visit us at
www.randomhouse.com/teachers

Library of Congress Cataloging-in-Publication Data
Brennan, Eileen (Eileen Bridget).
Dirtball Pete / by Eileen Brennan. – 1st ed.
    p. cm.
Summary: No matter how hard he tries, Dirtball Pete is always a mess, and even after his mother
scrubs him clean for a school recital to show others what a beautiful and special boy he is, he seems
destined to live up to his name.
ISBN 978-0-375-83425-7 (trade) – ISBN 978-0-375-93425-4 (lib. bdg.)
[1. Cleanliness–Fiction. 2. Pageants–Fiction. 3. Humorous stories.] I. Title.
PZ7.B75147 Dir 2010
[E]–dc22
2006022433

MANUFACTURED IN MALAYSIA
10 9 8 7 6 5 4 3 2 1
First Edition